BASEBALL LEGENDS

Hank Aaron
Grover Cleveland Alexander
Ernie Banks
Albert Belle
Johnny Bench
Yogi Berra
Barry Bonds
Roy Campanella
Roger Clemens
Roberto Clemente
Ty Cobb
Dizzy Dean
Joe DiMaggio
Bob Feller
Lou Gehrig
Bob Gibson
Ken Griffey, Jr.
Rogers Hornsby
Randy Johnson
Walter Johnson
Chipper Jones
Sandy Koufax
Life in the Minor Leagues
Greg Maddux

Mickey Mantle
Christy Mathewson
Willie Mays
Mark McGwire
Stan Musial
Mike Piazza
Cal Ripken, Jr.
Brooks Robinson
Frank Robinson
Jackie Robinson
Pete Rose
Babe Ruth
Nolan Ryan
Mike Schmidt
Tom Seaver
Duke Snider
Warren Spahn
Casey Stengel
Frank Thomas
Honus Wagner
Larry Walker
Ted Williams
Carl Yastrzemski
Cy Young

Chelsea House Publishers

Huntingdon Area
Middle School Library
Huntingdon, Pa.

BASEBALL LEGENDS

RANDY JOHNSON

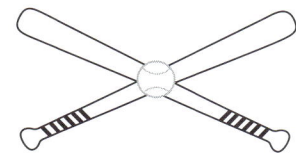

Mike Bonner

Introduction by
Jim Murray

Senior Consultant
Earl Weaver

CHELSEA HOUSE PUBLISHERS
Philadelphia

This book is dedicated to the memory of my father-in-law Fred Kleinheksel, a devoted family man and major league baseball fan who passed away in 1997. Fred loved his wife and children and was loved by them in return.

Produced by Choptank Syndicate, Inc.
Editor and Picture Researcher: Norman L. Macht
Production Coordinator and Editorial Assistant: Mary E. Hull
Design and Production: Lisa Hochstein

CHELSEA HOUSE PUBLISHERS

Editor in Chief: Stephen Reginald
Managing Editor: James Gallagher
Production Manager: Pamela Loos
Art Director: Sara Davis
Director of Photography: Judy L. Hasday
Senior Production Editor: Lisa Chippendale
Publishing Coordinator: James McAvoy
Cover Design and Digital Illustration: Keith Trego

Cover Photos: AP/Wide World Photos

© 1999 by Chelsea House Publishers,
a division of Main Line Book Co. All rights reserved.
Printed and bound in the United States of America.

The Chelsea House World Wide Web site
address is http://www.chelseahouse.com

First Printing

1 3 5 7 9 8 6 4 2

Library of Congress Cataloging-in-Publication Data

Bonner, Mike, 1951-
    Randy Johnson / Mike Bonner; introduction by Jim Murray;
    senior consultant, Earl Weaver
       p. cm.—(Baseball legends)
    Includes bibliographical references (p.) and index.
    Summary: A biography of the Seattle Mariner pitcher who won the
    Cy Young Award in 1995.
    ISBN 0-7910-5158-7 (hc). — ISBN 0-7910-5454-3 (pb).
    1. Johnson, Randy, 1963–   —Juvenile literature. 2. Baseball players—United
States—Biography—Juvenile literature.
[1. Johnson, Randy, 1963– . 2. Baseball players.] I. Weaver, Earl, 1930-   .
II. Title. III. Series.
GV865.J599B66 1999
796.357'092—dc21   98-18222
    [B]   CIP
                                                                 AC

CONTENTS

WHAT MAKES A STAR 6
Jim Murray

CHAPTER 1
THE BIG UNIT DIALS IN 9

CHAPTER 2
GROWING UP—
AND UP—AND UP 15

CHAPTER 3
FROM THE MINORS TO MONTREAL 21

CHAPTER 4
STANDING TALL IN SEATTLE 29

CHAPTER 5
THE PENNANT DRIVE 37

CHAPTER 6
THE ROAD BACK HOME 47

CHRONOLOGY 59

STATISTICS 60

FURTHER READING 61

INDEX 62

What Makes a Star

Jim Murray

No one has ever been able to explain to me the mysterious alchemy that makes one man a .350 hitter and another player, more or less identical in physical makeup, hard put to hit .200. You look at an Al Kaline, who played with the Detroit Tigers from 1953 to 1974. He was pale, stringy, almost poetic-looking. He always seemed to be struggling against a bad case of mononucleosis. But with a bat in his hands, he was King Kong. During his career, he hit 399 home runs, rapped out 3,007 hits, and compiled a .297 batting average.

Form isn't the reason. The first time anybody saw Roberto Clemente step into the batter's box for the Pittsburgh Pirates, the best guess was that Clemente would be back in Double A ball in a week. He had one foot in the bucket and held his bat at an awkward angle—he looked as though he couldn't hit an outside pitch. A lot of other ballplayers may have had a better-looking stance. Yet they never led the National League in hitting in four different years, the way Clemente did.

Not every ballplayer is born with the ability to hit a curveball. Nor is exceptional hand-eye coordination the key to heavy hitting. Big league locker rooms are filled with players who have all the attributes, save one: discipline. Every baseball man can tell you a story about a pitcher who throws a ball faster than anyone has ever seen but who has no control on or *off* the field.

The Hall of Fame is full of people who transformed themselves into great ballplayers by working at the sport, by studying the game, and making sacrifices. They're overachievers—and winners. If you want to find them, just watch the World Series. Or simply read about New York Yankee great Lou Gehrig; Ted Williams, "the Splendid Splinter" of the Boston Red Sox; or the Dodgers' strikeout king, Sandy Koufax.

A pitcher *should* be able to win a lot of ballgames with a 98-miles-per-hour fastball. But what about the pitcher who wins 20 games a year with a fastball so slow that you can catch it with your teeth? Bob Feller of the Cleveland Indians got into the Hall of Fame with a blazing fastball that glowed in the dark. National League star Grover Cleveland Alexander got there with a pitch that took considerably longer to reach the plate; but when it did arrive, the pitch was exactly where Alexander wanted it to be—and the last place the batter expected it to be.

There are probably more players with exceptional ability who didn't make it to the major leagues than there are who did. A number of great hitters, bored with fielding practice, had to be dropped from their team because their home-run production didn't make up for their lapses in the field. And then there are players like Brooks Robinson of the Baltimore Orioles, who made himself into a human vacuum cleaner at third base because he knew that working hard to become an expert fielder would win him a job in the big leagues.

A star is not something that flashes through the sky. That's a comet. Or a meteor. A star is something you can steer ships by. It stays in place and gives off a steady glow; it is fixed, permanent. A star works at being a star.

And that's how you tell a star in baseball. He shows up night after night and takes pride in how brightly he shines. He's Willie Mays running so hard his hat keeps falling off; Ty Cobb sliding to stretch a single into a double; Lou Gehrig, after being fooled in his first two at-bats, belting the next pitch off the light tower because he's taken the time to study the pitcher. Stars never take themselves for granted. That's why they're stars.

1
THE BIG UNIT DIALS IN

Standing atop the pitcher's mound on the night of May 23, 1997, Randy Johnson gave the opposing batter an icy glare. Fans at Royals Stadium in Kansas City were enjoying the night and the game, as their Royals had jumped ahead of Johnson's Seattle Mariners 4–0 in the third inning.

It had not been an easy road for the 6' 10" left-hander to reach this point. When he was young he had grown so tall so quickly he towered over the other kids his age, beginning in elementary school. His height made him the object of a lot of teasing, some of it mean.

As an athlete, his size gave him some advantages, but it also presented problems in coordination that he had to work hard to overcome. He could always throw hard, but it took him years to get his fastball under enough control to become a winning pitcher. His failure to keep his explosive temper under control cost him his first promotion to the major leagues.

His father, whom he idolized, had been his earliest coach and biggest supporter. His father's premature death was a blow that Randy never fully recovered from.

Johnson's windup is tight for such a big man, with his arms close to his body as he throws out his right leg and pushes off his left. The throwing motion is nearly sidearm.

Like most pitchers, Randy Johnson is off-limits to reporters on days he is to start. But after games and on days he doesn't work, he is usually willing to field questions. Here Johnson answers questions after being suspended for three days for throwing at Cleveland Indians' outfielder Kenny Lofton on April 15, 1998.

Eventually he had become the most dominant pitcher in the game. His fastball had been clocked at 100 miles per hour. His whiplike delivery and occasional wildness inspired many left-handed batters to seek a seat on the bench when he pitched. In 1995 he had been almost unbeatable, winning 18 against only two losses and earning the Cy Young Award.

But now Johnson was recovering from surgery for a herniated disk in his back that threatened to end his career. At 33, the Big Unit had become a big question mark. His 1996 season had ended on May 6; the operation took place on September 11. Nine months later he still suffered stiffness and pain.

Johnson and the Mariners were holding their breath, hoping that he could regain the strength required to sustain him through a long season. When the 1997 season began, Johnson had pitched well enough to compile a 5–1 record, thanks to Seattle's scoring a lot of runs for him. But the Mariners' overall pitching picture was a shambles. From opening day the bullpen had been regularly bombed. No lead seemed safe. The team desperately needed Johnson to come through for them.

By the end of three innings in Kansas City, however, things did not look good. On the mound, Johnson struggled with stiffness. Following each of his pitches, he felt a slight grab in his back.

Then the Seattle bats woke up. First baseman Paul Sorrento belted a two-run home run. Jay Buhner followed with another homer and the Mariners led 6–4. The lead gave Johnson the lift he needed. The pain and stiffness in his back were still there, but somehow they didn't feel so bad. He pitched with renewed power and authority, holding the Royals scoreless while ringing up 10 strikeouts in the 8–4 win.

After the game the Seattle coaching staff was upbeat for a change. "Randy really turned it around," manager Lou Piniella said. "Those home runs picked him up, picked everybody up."

Johnson was quick to credit his teammates with giving him the inspiration he needed. "Jay and Paul had big hits and they gave me a second chance," he said. "I've got to start dialing myself in sooner in these games. This was my third bad start and I'm just not as locked in as I have to be, fighting myself mentally and physically."

Five days later, Johnson started in Seattle's Kingdome against the Texas Rangers, determined to dial himself in early and often. The team needed an outstanding performance. A victory would cut the Rangers' American League West lead to a single game.

Standing beside the plate, batter Damon Buford cut the air with a few practice swings and waited for Johnson to throw. The streaking pitch dropped wickedly and cut across the center of the plate for a strike. A pair of blinding fastballs followed in quick succession. Strikeout. Another Ranger stepped in to face Johnson. Another strikeout.

Mixing his fastball with sharp sliders and curves, Johnson struck out 15 in eight innings for a 5–0 win. "A STRIKING PERFORMANCE" read the headline in the next day's *Seattle Times*.

"Randy was prepared tonight," Lou Piniella said. "There was no question about it. We needed a big performance from Randy and we got it."

"A game like this is nice," Johnson said. "I've done it before. But to me it's more satisfying because I'm coming back from back surgery. It's more gratifying, not so much to strike people out, but to go deep into the game. I knew that I needed to pitch a good game. It was reassuring to me that I could get out of the bad little streak I was in."

Johnson went on to win seven in a row. On June 2, he stretched his endurance to the limit, pitching his first complete game in almost two years while shutting out Toronto, 2–0.

Despite missing four games in August with tendonitis in the middle finger of his throwing hand, he became Seattle's first 20-game winner. Hitters batted a league-leading .193 against him.

He was second in the league in earned run average, wins, strikeouts, and the Cy Young voting (to Roger Clemens). He finished the season with exactly 2,000 career strikeouts, the 49th pitcher to reach that level.

Johnson had gone from question mark to solid pitcher. Thanks to his doctors and a will to win that was second to none, Randy Johnson had finally dialed himself in. And the American League knew that the Big Unit was back.

2
GROWING UP— AND UP—AND UP

Warm Santa Ana winds blow down from the foothills of the Sierra mountains to the town of Livermore, California. During the 1970s, propeller-driven windmills were built on the hillsides to take advantage of the winds and provide electricity to the community of 48,000 people 40 miles southeast of San Francisco.

Randall David Johnson was born to Carol and Rollen "Bud" Johnson on September 10, 1963, in the town of Walnut Creek, California. The youngest of six children, Randy was very small when the family moved to Livermore, about 45 miles away.

But Randy did not stay small for very long. By the sixth grade he was already six feet tall, towering over all the other kids in his class. Years later, Randy admitted being sensitive about his height. "I used to be a real outgoing person when I was younger. But then I started getting noticed a lot because of my height. I felt like I was in a three-ring circus and I didn't know how to handle it."

In school Randy was something of a rowdy, often getting into trouble with his teachers and other adults for his loud, wild antics. He had a

Randy Johnson was no blazing success when he joined the University of Southern California Trojans in 1982. He had difficulty adjusting to the academic demands and to being away from home for the first time.

As a junior in high school, Randy was always the easiest to spot in a crowd. In case you can't pick him out of this Livermore team photo, he is in the center of the the back row. Coach Eric Hoff is at the left end of the back row.

small group of close friends and enjoyed playing the drums and listening to music, but socially he felt awkward and out of place.

Fortunately for Randy, other members of his family were also tall, which helped him accept his height. His father, a 6' 6" security officer, played senior softball and had been a ski jumper in his native Minnesota. Whenever Randy pitched, from Little League through high school, he always looked for his father in the stands before throwing his first pitch, and Bud Johnson rarely let him down.

Ignoring the pain in his arthritic knees, Bud Johnson crouched in the backyard and played catch with Randy, working with his son to try to smooth out the kinks that very tall pitchers often have to overcome.

Randy was so devoted to his father he copied Bud's ways of walking and talking and many of his mannerisms. Despite Randy's size, his mother called him "Sweet Pea."

Randy's height made him eagerly sought for the basketball team at school, but it helped him as much on the baseball field. His long arms zoomed the ball past Little League hitters like a blur. The only problem was that he couldn't always make the ball go where he wanted it to go. Observers began to comment that Randy had little control, on or off the field.

In the ninth grade, Randy made the school basketball and baseball teams, eventually earning a letter in tennis as well. When he pitched for the Livermore junior varsity, opposing players tried to rattle him by calling him names like "long-necked geek." If Randy let their taunts get to him, his pitching suffered and his coach had to take him out of the game.

But Randy's father saw big league potential in his son and encouraged him to overcome his mental and physical problems on the mound. Randy's pitching blossomed under the guidance of his high school coach, Eric Hoff.

"Randy had to have perfect mechanics because of his height," Hoff said. "I also told him to stay inside himself and focus on a good attitude whatever happened."

Using Randy as a starter, Hoff's Livermore Cowboys became a powerhouse in the East Bay Athletic Conference. By now Randy was 6' 5" and

Randy Johnson poses with the Livermore Cowboys pitching staff in his senior year: Ken Higby (8), Steve Fallow (19), Wade Wondon (17), and Johnson (20).

USC coach Rod Dedeaux had sent many players to the major leagues, including Hall of Fame pitcher Tom Seaver, so Livermore High coach Eric Hoff thought USC was the best place for Randy to grow as a pitcher.

still growing. He was virtually invincible, striking out 10 or more hitters regularly. In his senior year he fanned 121 in 66 innings and pitched a perfect game in his final start.

Major league scouts had reached the same conclusion as Randy's dad: Randy had big league potential. The Atlanta Braves selected him in the third round of the 1982 draft after his graduation.

But Randy's dad and coach Eric Hoff felt that Randy needed to mature and fill out physically before launching a professional career. Hoff believed that Randy would benefit by going to the University of Southern California, where coach Rod Dedeaux had built an outstanding program during his 40 years on the Los Angeles campus. But USC offered Randy only a partial basketball scholarship, and that wasn't good enough. Coach Hoff went to bat for Randy and persuaded them to come up with a full baseball scholarship instead.

Randy's initial period of adjustment to college was difficult. Away from home for the first time, he fought the homesickness and insecurity that confront many college freshmen. He struggled with his classes and on the practice field. Never a top student, he spent hours studying to keep up his grades.

The USC baseball team had finished sixth in the Pac 10 in the spring of 1982. They also played a fall schedule in the warm climate of southern California, and Randy was thrown into action immediately. But it was too much of a strain on his arm. He worked only 17 innings before a sore arm sidelined him.

Randy began taking classes that appealed to him. He developed an interest in photography and became a fine arts major. Fellow students began to notice the exceptionally tall young man who went everywhere carrying a camera. He took pictures for the student newspaper and for a local rock music magazine.

In the spring, his arm healed, Randy worked to adjust to the college game's smaller strike zone and more selective hitters. Now at full height of 6' 10", his long left arm whipping the ball from a sidearm angle, he overpowered the opposition. When he lost, it was wildness that cost him.

As a sophomore, Randy had a 5–3 record and led USC to the College World Series, where they were eliminated in the first round. Scouts continued to follow his progress closely, impressed with his speed and not discouraged by his lack of control.

In his junior year he walked more batters than he struck out. But many young left-handers were wild. Some overcame it and had Hall of Fame careers. Others never did. The scouts believed that any southpaw who could throw as hard as Randy did was worth taking a chance on.

At the end of his junior year in 1985, Randy was once again eligible for the draft. This time, when the Montreal Expos took him in the second round, Randy felt that he was ready to become a professional pitcher.

3
FROM THE MINORS TO MONTREAL

The Montreal Expos sent their new pitcher to their Class A farm team in Jamestown, New York. To help refine his skills, they assigned coach Bud Janus to find ways of getting the most out of Randy's power while minimizing his bad habits.

The switch to pro ball revealed some of the same problems Randy had faced in college. The strike zone shrinks at each higher level as hitters' skills improve; they don't swing at as many bad pitches. Johnson had to hone his control. He walked 24 in the 27 innings he pitched before going down with a sore arm.

The Expos were concerned about Johnson's physical stamina. His slender frame didn't seem to be able to handle the demands of a full season. They recommended a workout program to add weight and muscle. The work in the weight room paid off. Johnson reported for the 1986 season stronger and heavier.

Assigned to the West Palm Beach Eagles in the Class A Florida State League, Johnson chalked up 133 strikeouts in 119 innings with an 8–7 record. That earned him a promotion to Jacksonville in the AA Southern League. Players reaching this

As a rookie with the Montreal Expos in 1989, Johnson was aided by a reputation for wildness that made hitters nervous about digging in too firmly at the plate.

Johnson broke in with the Class A Jamestown, New York, Expos in 1985. As always, he stood head and shoulders above his teammates in the center of the middle row.

level were among the top prospects. Johnson had filled out to 240 pounds. His fastball had more movement on it. But he was still walking as many as he struck out.

Johnson had everything he needed to succeed; he just had to learn how to harness and drive it. Hitters couldn't hit his stuff, but they didn't have to in order to beat him. On May 2 he gave up nine walks to the Huntsville Stars. Ten days later he issued another nine free passes to the Birmingham Barons, including four in the fourth inning.

Rico Petrocelli, a 12-year major league player who was managing the Barons, said, "I was impressed with Johnson's stuff, his easy delivery. All of a sudden, bang, it's by you. When he gets his control, he's going to be an exceptional big league pitcher. That's just a matter of time and hard work."

But the Birmingham batters could manage only one hit off Johnson's fastball that night and he escaped with a 6–2 win.

"He was sensational when he had to be," Petrocelli said. "As I was looking at him from the third base coach's box, he reminded me of [Hall of Famer] Sandy Koufax when he was that age. . . . He was a little wild, too."

After the game, Johnson felt confident that he was making progress, despite the nine walks. "The fact that they got only one hit tonight shows they're not hitting me well," he said. "And the walks had been going down the last two starts. I was getting more confident. I just hope tonight was just one of those things you have to get out of your system."

The Jacksonville pitching coach, Joe Kerrigan, was 6' 5" himself, so he knew some of the challenges Johnson faced with his mechanics. Kerrigan worked with Randy to add variety to his pitches. In countless individual sessions, Kerrigan taught Johnson that his control would improve if he let up a little on his fastball. He urged Johnson to use his curve and slider more often. Kerrigan was teaching him to become a pitcher, not just a thrower.

The breakthrough came on the night of June 8 against the Greenville Braves. Using what he called his "B-fastball," Johnson threw with less velocity. He walked five and threw two wild pitches, but that was an improvement. Besides, he kept the walks scattered and did not go into a sustained lapse of control. The 5–4 victory, his first in four starts, boosted his record to 7–1.

"The B-fastball is a kind of reserved fastball, but I get it over," he said. "When I use it, I'm more of a thinker. I'm a pitcher, rather than a thrower. My last couple of outings, I had to be a pitcher."

Coach Kerrigan was also encouraged. "He has more confidence in his slider on 2-and-1 and 3-and-1 counts," he said. "The breaking ball

This is what Southern League hitters saw when Randy Johnson delivered a pitch in 1987. The hitter had less time than the blink of an eye to react. Pitching for Jacksonville, he held opposing batters to a .204 average.

helps bring his delivery back in sync and he is understanding that more."

Johnson, a weak hitter, also walked and had a single in the game, in which teammate Larry Walker, later a National League MVP with the Colorado Rockies, had three hits and stole three bases.

But Johnson's progress was not steady. On August 19 he walked the first two batters he faced, then grooved a fastball that disappeared for a three-run homer. Two innings later he hit a batter, then walked a few more to force in a run. He kept walking into trouble all night.

Johnson finished 1987 with an 11–8 record and a league-leading 163 strikeouts. More important, he did not lead the league in walks.

Players and fans alike were enthralled by the speed of his fastball. In pre-game clinics for kids, hundreds lined up for a chance to demonstrate their windup and get tips from the fireballer.

In the minor leagues Johnson developed some of the traits that would earn him a reputation for eccentric behavior. He played pranks on teammates and fans. Once he pretended to be waving to the fans when suddenly a fake arm flew out of his sleeve.

The world blew hot and cold for Johnson's sensitive soul. Like many gifted individuals, he could be a creature of moods. It irked him whenever a public address announcer would tell the crowd that Johnson was the tallest player in baseball, making it sound, he complained, "like I was some sort of freak."

Wherever his team played, photographers invariably asked him to pose with the shortest

Joe Kerrigan practices his "mean" look as a relief pitcher for Montreal and Baltimore in the 1970s. The 6′ 5″ pitcher knew about the problems tall pitchers have in developing smooth mechanics, which helped him as Johnson's pitching coach in the minor leagues.

player on the field, as if it was an original idea. It became his pet peeve in the minors.

Johnson's mother chalked up his behavior to boredom. "I think he spent too much time with nothing to do," she said.

On game days, Johnson had a set routine. He got up early and headed to a restaurant for a stack of pancakes, scrambled eggs, and milk. He read the newspapers, carefully skipping the sports section. After breakfast he returned to his room, turned on the TV, and banged his drums for an hour. Then he went to the ballpark.

Johnson also picked up a superstition that required him to sleep with his head at the foot of the bed on nights before he pitched. But one time he fell asleep while watching TV with his head at the head of the bed and still won the next day. That cured him. "I don't have any superstitions anymore," he said.

Other pitchers watched him with envy. "What I wouldn't give to have his arm for one game," said Brian Holman, another young Expos prospect. "I'd spend that game scaring people to death. As a left-handed hitter, you couldn't pay me enough to stand in there against him."

Holman and Johnson were teammates at AAA Indianapolis in 1988. "One day," Holman related, "Randy drilled a hitter with a fastball. The batter started toward the mound. Randy screamed at him, 'Don't mess with me. I'll take your life.' The guy went right to first base."

Johnson's emotional fuse could blow at any time. On the night of June 14, in Indianapolis with Montreal officials scouting him for a possible promotion, he was on the mound when a batter hit a line drive right at him. The ball banged his left arm and bounced away. The pain was intense and Johnson feared that his pitching career was over. He stormed off the mound in tears and punched a bat rack, breaking his right hand.

X-rays showed his valuable left arm was bruised but not broken. However, the broken right hand sidelined him for six weeks, and ended any hopes of a mid-season promotion.

When the Indianapolis season ended, the Expos called Johnson up to the big leagues. He made his first start on September 15, a 9–4 win over Pittsburgh. Johnson won three of his four starts without a loss, striking out 25 and walking only seven, and went home for the winter confident of a long future in Montreal.

4

STANDING TALL IN SEATTLE

A 1989 pre-season newspaper roundup named Randy Johnson the top rookie in the National League East and the most frightening pitcher in all baseball. Speed alone doesn't scare big league hitters; they can hit a fastball. It's the scatter-armed flame-throwers that make them nervous about digging in at the plate. Johnson's reputation came with him and it was well documented: he had walked 378 batters in 400 innings in the minor leagues.

Randy Johnson didn't last long in Montreal in the spring of 1989. A disappointing 0–4 start reflected his continuing control problems. He was what pitching coaches call a "spinner," moving around in his delivery with erratic results. In 30 innings he walked 26 with 26 strikeouts, before the Expos sent him back to Indianapolis.

Joe Kerrigan still believed in Johnson. He continued to work on improving the lefty's mechanics. In three starts Johnson cut his walks to nine while fanning 17. But the gap between the minors and the big leagues is a wide one. Montreal officials began to wonder if Johnson would ever be able to cross it and become a consistent winner.

Johnson called his father after every game he pitched. When his father died in 1992, Johnson said, "My whole life was ready to crumble inside of me." Before each game, Johnson says a prayer in which he mentions his dad. "Every time I go out there, I bring him out there. There's always games when I just look back there behind home plate and see him watching."

Meanwhile, the Seattle Mariners were looking for pitching help. Since the team had entered the American League in 1977, they had never finished higher than fourth. They decided to trade their top pitcher, Mark Langston, to Montreal for three young hurlers: Brian Holman, Gene Harris, and Randy Johnson.

Johnson was the first of the new Mariners to see action, facing the always-dangerous New York Yankees in New York. Expectations were low. The Mariners were in the midst of a skid when the three new pitchers arrived. They had gone 1–6 on the road trip that brought them to Yankee Stadium. The latest defeat had come on May 29, a 6–3 loss to the Yankees. Five Seattle pitchers had failed in that game.

The next day Johnson started and allowed only two runs and six hits in six innings. He walked three and struck out six in the 3–2 win. "I think a lot of people were waiting for me to be wild," he said after the game. "I think I got a lot of first pitch strikes because they were waiting for me to fall behind."

Watching from center field, Ken Griffey Jr. gaped at his new teammate, the tallest man ever to pitch in the major leagues. "Johnson's so tall," Griffey marveled, "sometimes it seemed like he was just handing the ball to our catcher."

Struggling to stay afloat, the Mariners were not yet a good team. Johnson's debut gave them a shot in the arm, but it was not enough. His 7–9 record the rest of the year was better than the Mariners' sixth-place finish.

In 1990 Johnson continued to improve. On May 1 he became the first left-handed pitcher to strike out six-time AL batting champion Wade Boggs three times in a game.

A month later, on June 2, he started against the Detroit Tigers at the Kingdome. The Tigers had a powerful lineup, led by slugger Cecil Fielder. Power pitchers give up a lot of home runs; Johnson had thrown 12 so far, most in the major leagues. He had to make some adjustments. Before the game he and his catcher, Scott Bradley, decided that he had to throw his fastball inside all night to escape the long ball.

Randy Johnson tips his cap to the Kingdome crowd in the middle of the ninth inning on September 26, 1993, after becoming the eighth pitcher in American League history to strike out at least 300 batters in a season.

Johnson started slowly, issuing walks but no hits to the patient hitters. In the sixth inning he walked the bases loaded with two outs, then fanned Chet Lemon to end the threat. He got stronger after that and kept the Tigers off balance.

"He was throwing completely backwards," said Tiger Tony Phillips. "He was throwing fastballs when he should have been throwing breaking balls."

In other words, he was pitching with his head as well as his arm.

Johnson took a 2–0 lead into the ninth and got two quick outs. With the crowd of 20,004 standing and screaming, the 97-mph pitch he threw to strike out Mike Heath to end the game was his fastest of the night. He had pitched the first no-hitter in Kingdome history, but, he said later, "I didn't know how to react. I just stood there."

Five days later in Chicago he pitched another complete game, striking out 10 in a 2–1 win. Johnson went 5–0 in June and was named the AL Pitcher of the Month.

By the All-Star break he had a 9–3 record and was chosen for the All-Star team but did not get into the game. Despite his final 14–11 record, the Mariners could rise no higher than fifth in the AL West.

As tough as he was to hit, Johnson was equally hard for his teammates to understand. It seemed as if he didn't want anything to do with any of them. "I'm a very moody person," he admitted. "I live in my own little world. I don't like people talking to me."

The 83–79 record the Mariners posted in 1991 was the first winning year in their 15-year history, but they again finished fifth. Despite back problems that hampered him early in the season, Johnson led the team with 13 wins, was second in the league with 228 strikeouts, but also led the league with 152 walks. He was consistently inconsistent.

Help sometimes comes from unexpected sources. Johnson was still a "spinner;" his windup,

Catchers look up to Randy Johnson in more ways than one. Here Dave Valle congratulates the Big Unit after Johnson pitched a one-hitter against Oakland.

release point, and follow-through were jerky and erratic, varying from pitch to pitch. His height made it awkward for him to hold runners on base. One day in 1992 the Texas Rangers were in Seattle. Pitchers often study other pitchers, analyzing their deliveries and patterns. Nolan Ryan and Texas pitching coach Tom House watched Johnson throwing in the bullpen. They could see that Johnson was having trouble with his control, and exchanged a few thoughts on how they would correct his flaws.

When he was finished, Johnson expressed his disgust at his own performance to them. They offered some advice, especially on driving toward the plate in his follow-through. Johnson was ready to listen; after all, Ryan was the premier power pitcher in baseball, and House was one of the top pitching teachers. House talked about his mechanics. Ryan helped him with the mental part: setting up hitters and not letting walks upset him.

Johnson became the toughest pitcher in the league to hit, but he also hit more batters—18—than any other pitcher, and led in walks as well as strikeouts. During one two-month stretch, Johnson lost eight in a row, due mainly to a feeble Seattle lineup that scored few runs for him. He finished 12–14 for the seventh-place Mariners.

All those stats became unimportant to him on Christmas day 1992 when his father died of heart problems. Randy was not home at the time and had no chance to say goodbye.

"The day after, I drove home with my mom, back to the house where my parents live," he later told a Seattle writer, "and I remember crying in bed that night, weeping because my dad is dead.

"From that day on, I got a lot more strength and determination to be the best player I could be, and not to get sidetracked and not to look at things as pressure, but as challenges.

"What my dad went through was pressure. That was life and death. [Baseball] is a game."

But Johnson's first reaction to his father's death was to quit baseball. He turned to his mother and his girlfriend, Lisa, for advice. They urged him to stay in the game, using his father's memory for renewed inspiration and motivation.

5

THE PENNANT DRIVE

In 1993 Lou Piniella became the Mariners' manager. Piniella knew what it took to win. He had played in four World Series with the Yankees and managed Cincinnati to a World Championship in 1990.

Piniella was disturbed that Johnson seemed more concerned at times with racking up strikeouts than winning. One day Johnson gave up eight runs in less than two innings. When Piniella went out to take the ball from him, Johnson did not wait for him, but walked off the mound before the manager got there. That irked Piniella.

The next day Piniella called Johnson into his office and suggested a change of attitude might help him realize his potential better.

"That made me look in the mirror," Johnson said later. "It was a learning lesson and after that I didn't have any more games like that. Out of my next 10 starts I won eight of them. I became a little more determined."

Johnson led the majors in strikeouts with 308, cut his walks by one-third, and equaled Mark Langston's Mariners club record of 19 wins. On June 16 he reached the ultimate goal for a pitcher

Johnson works on his fielding as well as his pitching. Here he signals to catcher Ivan Rodriguez to throw to second base on an attempted sacrifice bunt during the 1995 All-Star Game.

plagued by wildness, striking out 15 Kansas City Royals without walking a single batter in a 6–3 win.

Under new manager Lou Piniella, the Mariners began to improve, finishing fourth. Johnson's 19–8 record and 10 complete games placed him second in the Cy Young Award voting.

His father's death had made Randy Johnson a more serious, focused person. His marriage to Lisa in November 1993 added more stability to his life. Before his marriage, he had warned her that ballplayers, especially moody pitchers, were not always easy to live with. She would have to learn to give him plenty of space on the days he pitched.

Although 1993 had been a big year for Randy Johnson, 1994 promised to be bigger still. Beginning on May 25, he threw three consecutive shutouts, the last coming on June 4. On August 11 he won his 13th game, striking out his 15th Oakland hitter of the night on what turned out to be the last pitch thrown in the 1994 season. The next day, the players, unable to reach agreement with the owners on a new contract, went on strike. Eventually the rest of the season and the World Series were canceled.

On December 28 the Johnsons' first child, a daughter, Samantha, was born. Becoming a father helped Johnson grow. He was determined, he said, not to be "flaky" anymore. He would be a warrior on the field and a responsible, caring adult the rest of the time.

"When my daughter Samantha was born, I didn't care if I played baseball again," he said later. "I would do whatever I could to support my family. You can't be selfish anymore. It made me understand how my mom and dad made sacrifices for us, too. Hopefully, I can be half the dad my father was and raise my family the same way my parents raised me. I'm excited about doing that."

As Johnson matured, his style on the mound changed. Formerly, after notching a strikeout, he would sometimes dismiss the batter with a wave of his hand. Now he pounded his chest with his glove in a gesture of respect.

Johnson's popularity also grew in the Northwest Empire that followed the Mariners. Fans turned out in greater numbers at the Kingdome whenever he pitched. One fan wrote a song based on the rock tune "American Woman":

"Randy Johnson. . . hey, what you make? Randy Johnson. . . racking up the Ks."

Fans arrived at the ballpark wearing Johnson's number 51 jersey, woolly fake mustaches, and long hair. The boy who had been called a "geek" now had thousands of people in one of America's most fashionable cities copying his style.

Thousand of fans swarmed around the bullpen to watch him warm up or throw in practice sessions. Commenting on the excitement at the Kingdome when he pitched, Johnson said, "It's more like a festival, or it might be like a Rolling Stones show."

The attention Johnson gained from his baseball success had unexpected benefits. Johnson discovered that his status as a celebrity allowed him the opportunity to meet and become friends with some of his heavy metal music heroes, such as Geddy Lee of Rush and Chris DeGarmo of Queensryche. They even invited him to play the drums with the band during studio sound checks. His best friend among the musicians

Ken Griffey Jr. makes a leaping catch of a fly ball before crashing into the wall on May 26, 1995. The impact broke two bones in Griffey's wrist, sidelining him for more than two months.

was Kim Thayll, guitarist for the rock group Soundgarden.

Johnson's family and photography also occupied his time. Using his two pro-quality Pentaxes, Johnson explored the cities where he pitched through his camera lens, capturing black and white images.

One photograph that struck a chord with art lovers was his famous "car in the dumpster" shot. Few people who pass by a garbage dumpster are tall enough to see what's inside. Randy Johnson could. One day he peered over a high rim and saw a car neatly fitted within the confines of an industrial dumpster. Johnson shot the scene, producing his most admired photo.

At an exhibition in Seattle, Johnson raised $14,000 from the sale of his pictures for charity. Modest about his work, he found similarities between taking pictures and baseball. "In both activities, you have to stay focused," he said with a smile.

His work with local charities earned him the Mariners' "Care Community Service Award" in 1996. He helped Seattle's homeless through the Union Gospel Mission, chaired the team's "Ks for Kids" program for the Boys and Girls Clubs, and raised money for cystic fibrosis research.

Johnson also reached out to his teammates as a friend and mentor. He took Jay Buhner along on a Times Square photo shoot, and started golfing with Mike Blowers, Chris Bosio, and Greg Hibbard. When other pitchers were going through slumps, Johnson began to approach them to offer support and encouragement.

In March 1995 the Seattle club owners announced plans to build a new stadium with public financing. After a losing record in 1994, the pressure was on the players to make a good showing to boost support for the new stadium. Otherwise, the team might be sold and moved to another city.

The players' strike ended in time to play a shortened 144-game schedule. The early weeks were up and down for Seattle, with a 10–10 record. On May 7 Johnson pitched an emotional game against the California Angels. The Angels loaded the bases with nobody out in the fifth inning. The next batter sent a tapper back to Johnson, who juggled it but threw to catcher Dan Wilson in time for the force-out. The second out came on a soft liner to second. The runners held. Johnson then struck out Rex Hudler for the third out.

When Hudler went down, Johnson shouted for joy and pounded his chest with his glove. Some of the Angels objected to Johnson's demonstration. "I heard him, his barking, after he punched me out," Hudler said. "I'll get him next time."

"I'm just animated," Johnson answered. "That was a key moment for me and for the team. I'm gifted that I'm a power pitcher who can turn it up and elevate myself for those situations that you have to rise to."

Disaster struck the Mariners on May 26. Ken Griffey Jr., the heart of the batting order, broke both bones in his wrist while snagging a deep fly against the outfield wall. The team's leading hitter would be out for more than two months. Lou Piniella told his players that every man would have to step up to fill the empty space.

"There's two ways we could have gone after Junior went down," Johnson said. "We could either fold and lose a lot of games before he came back, or the players could believe in themselves and try to get by with what we had."

Bad blood developed between the Yankees and Mariners in June when a high, inside fastball from Johnson struck Jim Leyritz on the wrist and bounced into his face. Leyritz went down and the benches cleared.

"Johnson better hope he doesn't see me out there [in the playoffs]," Leyritz said. "We'll take care of it one way or the other."

Johnson sought to play down the incident. saying the pitch just got away from him. He offered to meet Leyritz for lunch or, he joked, they could duel it out "1600s style, with either swords or pistols at 20 paces."

As the starter in the All-Star Game, Johnson pitched two innings but did not get a decision.

On July 31 the Mariners trailed the California Angels by 13 games in the AL West. Seattle and the rest of the division was left to scramble for the elusive wild card berth in the playoffs. After Ken Griffey Jr. rejoined the team on August 26, the Mariners put on a show for their screaming

Randy Johnson's lean, angular body is built along the lines of legendary fastballers Lefty Grove, shown here, and Walter Johnson. Grove dominated AL hitters for the pennant-winning Philadelphia Athletics 1929–1931. Walter Johnson won 416 games in 21 years for the Washington Senators.

fans, winning 17 of their last 22 games while the Angels went into a tailspin. Johnson was 7–0 in his last 10 starts. The two teams finished the season tied.

On October 2 Seattle hosted the one-game playoff for the AL West title. Johnson dominated the Angels with a three-hit, 12-K complete game for a 9–1 win.

Seattle lost the first two games of the Division Series to the Yankees in New York and came home one loss away from a hasty elimination. In the second game, New York outfielder Ruben Sierra hot-dogged his way around the bases after his game-winning homer, while TV cameras zeroed in on a steaming Ken Griffey Jr. in the Seattle dugout.

Johnson kept Seattle's hopes alive with a 7–4 win in Game 3, and four Seattle home runs won an 11–8 slugfest the next day to even the series. In the hard-fought finale, the score was 4–4 after eight innings. Johnson came in to pitch the ninth in relief, only the third time in his major league career that he had relieved. He was still pitching in the top of the 11th when he gave up the go-ahead run and it looked like the end of the line for the Mariners. But they came back to score twice in the bottom of the 11th to make Johnson a winner and advance to the ALCS against the Cleveland Indians.

Seattle won two games against the Indians, but their bats were stifled in the other four, and Cleveland went on to the World Series. Randy Johnson went home, where he learned that his 18–2 record, 2.48 earned run average, and 294 strikeouts had earned him the Cy Young Award, the first postseason honor ever won by a Seattle player.

On receiving the trophy, Johnson credited his wife and parents, invoking the memory of his father. "My father passed away in 1992 and that was the year my heart got a lot bigger," he said. "A lot of people have wondered why, all of a sudden, this transformation happened. It's a matter of maturity and . . . of dedicating myself to being the best."

The Mariners' success on the field saved the team for the city. The voters approved the financing of the new stadium, but by the time it was built Randy Johnson had other plans.

6
THE ROAD BACK HOME

The Arizona Diamondbacks had been awarded an expansion franchise in the National League to begin play in Phoenix in 1998. Randy Johnson had just built a home that included a huge exercise and workout room in Paradise Valley, about 20 minutes' drive from Phoenix, when he reported to the Mariners' spring training camp in Arizona in February 1996. There he confided to a Phoenix reporter, "I've got two years left [with Seattle] and then I'll be down playing with the Diamondbacks."

The idea of playing near his home, enabling him to spend more time with his young family, which added a son, Tanner Hollen, in April, appealed to Johnson.

Meanwhile, there was a pennant to be won in Seattle. But Johnson's aching back limited him to eight starts and a 5–0 record, and the Mariners narrowly missed making the playoffs without him.

At 33, Randy Johnson was a big question mark for the Mariners in 1997. The surgery he underwent to repair his herniated disk had been successful, but something could always go wrong. The rest of the pitching staff was even more up in the air. Following an 18–3 pasting on May 21, Lou

"He's the most dominating pitcher right now," said the Rockies' Dante Bichette in 1997. "When he came up he had that fastball and the strikeouts. But he didn't have that look in his eye. Now he's got that possessed look in his eye. If you just look at him, you could get intimidated."

Piniella said, "I'm disappointed and somewhat disgusted. I don't get easily discouraged but we've hit rock bottom."

In an interleague game against the Colorado Rockies in June, Johnson had his first opportunity to test his fastball against his former Jacksonville teammate, Larry Walker. A left-handed batter, Walker was having an MVP year with the Rockies. He was hitting .409 at the time. But the confrontation never happened; like many American League left-handed swingers, Walker chose to sit out the game rather than face Johnson.

Both players were chosen for the All-Star Game in July. Walker was elected as a starter by the fans, and Johnson was picked to start for the American League by manager Joe Torre of the Yankees. This time Walker had no choice. He had to hit against Johnson.

"Maybe I'll bat right-handed," Walker joked before the game.

Johnson joined in the spirit of the occasion. When Walker stepped gingerly into the batter's box in the second inning, Johnson wound up and fired a fastball that soared high over Walker's head and banged against the screen.

Looking scared but laughing to himself, Walker jumped across the plate, turned his batting helmet around, and stared at Johnson from the right-handers' position. "I didn't even know if I was allowed to do that," he said later.

After Johnson threw ball two, Walker went back to his normal batting stance and drew a walk.

Johnson later denied that his wild pitch had been intentional. "It was kind of humid out there. The ball slipped out of my hand. Since when have I mastered control? I'm sorry it happened to Larry. But if it had to happen, who's a more fitting guy to have it happen to?"

For Johnson, it was his fourth All-Star appearance without a decision.

After the break, the Mariners' trio of lefties— Johnson, Jeff Fassero, and Jamie Moyer— stepped forward and led the Mariners to the AL West championship. Moyer was 17–5 and Fassero 16–9.

And Johnson? Seldom free of pain while pitching, he had to get physical therapy after every start. Trainers wrapped up to 10 bags of ice around his midsection and on his left arm after he pitched. Between starts he worked out for two to three hours every day and took pain medication.

When he pitched at home and the Mariners were at bat, he lay down on the trainer's table with his feet propped high to ease the pressure on his back. On the road he stretched out on the floor.

Pitching coach Nardi Contreras said, "His intensity is pretty scary. I've never seen anyone as focused or determined as Randy Johnson."

Working with and around his pain, Randy Johnson gave the Mariners the best pitching performance in the team's history. He tied the league record with 16 straight wins going back to 1995 before losing a rain-interrupted game in Baltimore on May 8. Relying on two varieties of fastball and a pair of sliders, he reeled off 31 consecutive shutout innings, set a league record for left-handers with 19 strikeouts against Oakland, and won 20 games against 4 losses.

Randy Johnson had gained recognition as a complete pitcher, not just a thrower. He had a two-seam and four-seam fastball, a changeup, and an 88-mile-an-hour slider that other players nicknamed "Mr. Snappy."

"I go out there and have a game plan and throw a changeup and set up hitters and try to get ground balls so I can throw fewer pitches in a game," he said.

Johnson denied that he tried to strike out every hitter. "I like strikeouts and stuff but it's not what I'm about. It's not like I'm trying to go out there and do it. If I was trying to strike out people, how come I didn't strike out 20 . . . I was trying to strike out people when I knew I had 19 [against Oakland] and I couldn't do it."

The Mariners went into the Division Series against the AL East champion Baltimore Orioles full of optimism. The first two games of the best-of-five series would be played in the Kingdome. Their trio of southpaws was well rested. They had a powerful lineup in Alex Rodriguez, Ken Griffey Jr., Edgar Martinez, and Jay Buhner.

In Game 1 the Mariners hit three solo home runs off Orioles ace Mike Mussina, but Randy Johnson was not sharp. He gave up five runs in five innings and the Orioles coasted to a 9–3 win.

Game 2 was the same disappointing story. Seattle's starter and relievers gave up nine runs in another 9–3 loss. Now they would have to take three in a row in Baltimore to advance. Behind home runs by Jay Buhner and Paul Sorrento and the three-hit pitching of Jeff Fassero, they won Game 3, 4–2.

Game 4 was a rematch of the teams' aces, Johnson and Mussina. Johnson pitched well enough to win, giving up three runs and striking out 13, but Mussina was a little better, allowing just two hits in a 3–1 win that ended Seattle's season short of their goal again.

The Mariners had an option on Johnson for 1998, but Johnson's agents had told them during the 1997 season that Randy preferred to play for the Arizona Diamondbacks when the new team began play in '98. The Mariners exercised their option anyhow. Arizona would have to wait.

Beyond that, the Mariners remained silent throughout the fall of 1997 on their plans for Johnson's future. Despite his agents' indicating that the pitcher had his sights on Arizona, Johnson let it be known that he felt insulted and disrespected when the Mariners made no move to offer him a contract extension, as they had done for other players. He felt that, considering all he had done for the franchise, he deserved at least some show of interest in the team's retaining him.

Then, in November, at a press conference to announce that Ken Griffey Jr. had been named the AL Most Valuable Player, a reporter asked the Mariners' president, Chuck Armstrong, if the team intended to offer Johnson a contract extension. For the first time, the team admitted that they had no such plans, claiming that they did not have the money they knew it would take to satisfy him.

Johnson was still upset over the situation when he reported for spring training in February 1998. If the Mariners didn't want him beyond '98, he preferred to be traded before the season started. The Mariners did talk trade with other teams, but nothing happened. Johnson accused them of asking for not only players but "the Statue of Liberty" from the Yankees, and "a couple of players and Jacobs Field" from the Cleveland Indians.

His temper grew short as reporters continually peppered him with questions about trade rumors. In one spring training interview session that lasted less than a minute, he said that he felt good, his arm and back were healthy, and "I don't feel like talking anymore."

But the uncertainty and the persistent feeling that he was not appreciated by the team kept preying on his mind. He could not keep quiet about it. For every time he refused to talk about it, there were times when he aired his displeasure voluntarily.

"I'm not a piece of meat out there," he told a radio interviewer. "I have feelings and I want to be treated like anybody else. When I'm gone—and I'm going to be gone and not by my own choosing—the one thing I'll miss is the fans."

So it was an unhappy Randy Johnson who opened the season in Seattle. It wasn't long before the team was losing as often as they won and rumors began to circulate again that Johnson was on the trading block. He pitched poorly at times. Writers took shots at him, accusing him of letting down and of not caring whether the team won or lost. It seemed apparent to some observers that Johnson's heart was elsewhere.

Team management also came in for criticism, many fans and commentators wondering why they were making no effort to sign Johnson to a new contract. Except for Ken Griffey Jr., Randy Johnson was their franchise player. Amid the rancor and negative comments, the good will and optimism inspired by the 1995 and 1997 playoff appearances dissipated as the team floundered below .500.

With no chance of making the playoffs, and knowing that Johnson would be a free agent at the end of the season, the Mariners actively sought to deal Johnson to one of the contenders looking for a pitcher who might carry them to the world championship. With a trade, they would at least get something in return for him. Just before the trading deadline of July 31, the Houston Astros won the prize, sending four young minor leaguers to Seattle for Johnson. His record was 9–10, but the fans and his teammates, especially Ken Griffey Jr., Jay Buhner, and Alex Rodriguez, were sorry to see him go.

The Houston Astros and their fans, however, were delighted to see him come to the Astrodome. They were even more ecstatic when, two days after his long flight to Texas, he struck out 12 Pittsburgh Pirates in a 6–2 win.

"It's just fun to be back in the National League," said a smiling, relaxed Randy Johnson. "I've still got to learn the hitters and the ballparks, but that will come."

The last time Johnson had batted in a game was in 1989 with the Montreal Expos. In the American League the designated hitter replaced the pitcher in the batting order. The National League did not use the DH. Now he would have to pick up a bat again. He batted right-handed with a protective wrapping on his valuable left arm. Johnson had gotten two hits in his 16 at-bats at Montreal. In Houston he concentrated on practicing bunting to advance a runner rather than swinging away, but he still managed two hits in 32 at-bats. His career batting average at that point was .091.

The man who rode into Houston to take the Astros to the World Series immediately became

With Seattle, Johnson never swung a bat in a game. In Houston and then Arizona, with no DH in the National League, Johnson had to bat. "In Houston," he said, "people said it was kind of comical that the bat looked like a toothpick in my hands."

the center of attention throughout the city. He felt content to be wanted so much after the bitterness he had left in Seattle, but he admitted, "It does get a little overwhelming when you are driving to your hotel and kids are screaming at you out the window and you go to the mall and people are looking at you. But, eventually, I'll get old and my back will be bad, so now I'm just going to have fun with it."

He also admitted that the pressure to win sometimes bothered him. "Teammates rely on me too much. It's like when I'm pitching I can't make a mistake out there, and that's not right."

Still, he took it as a challenge, and responded by winning 10 games against one loss as the Astros won the NL Central Division. That put them into the Division Series against the San Diego Padres, who had an ace of their own in Kevin Brown.

Somehow it seemed to be Johnson's fate in postseason play to run into either the other team's ace at his best or a sudden departure of his own team's batting eye. It had happened in Seattle in 1995 and '97, and it happened again in '98. He gave up only two runs in each of his two starts against the Padres, but the Astros scored only one run in each game.

His season over, Johnson went home to await the birth of his third child, a daughter they named Willow, and to field what would likely be record-breaking offers for a pitcher who had won 62 games against 17 losses in the past four years, and had just led the majors in strikeouts for the fifth time with 329. He was 35, but he had demonstrated that he could overcome his chronic back problems and his arm was sound.

Although Anaheim, Texas, and the Los Angeles Dodgers made him comparable financial offers, there was little doubt that Randy Johnson still wanted to sign with the Diamondbacks, who had finished last in their debut season with a 65–97 record. On November 30 he signed a four-year $52 million contract that included such fringe benefits as a luxury suite at the Phoenix ballpark and season tickets to the NBA Suns games (the Suns were owned by the Diamondbacks' owner, Jerry Colangelo).

Johnson had always had an on-and-off relationship with the media. He knew that he had to face the cameras and writers after games

RANDY JOHNSON

Randy Johnson wraps a long-armed hug around his mother, who calls him "Sweet Pea," at the press conference announcing his signing with the Arizona Diamondbacks on December 2, 1998.

in which he pitched. On other days he might be friendly and chatty, or he might not feel like talking to anybody. But he had some rules that were firm, as one Phoenix TV reporter learned the day after Johnson signed.

When the reporter showed up uninvited at Johnson's home, he was told to get lost. "There are certain things that are dos and don'ts," Johnson explained, voicing a sentiment shared by most players. "Coming to my home is a don't. It's the only place I have to unwind, to have solitude. I don't feel my home is the place to do an interview."

The next day, with his mother, Carol Johnson, his wife, and two of his children looking on, Johnson told a press conference he did not expect to carry the Diamondbacks on his aching back to the World Series right away, but maybe they could be contenders in a year or two. "I'm not perfect," he said. "I don't walk on water.

"Baseball's my life," he concluded. "Been doing it since I was seven years old."

Whatever he said silently to his absent father, he did not reveal.

Chronology

1963	Born in Walnut Creek, California, on September 10.
1982	Enrolls at USC on full baseball scholarship.
1985	Selected in second round of draft by the Montreal Expos.
1988	Wins first major league start on September 15.
1989	Traded to Seattle Mariners.
1990	Pitches first Mariners no-hitter against Detroit on June 2.
1992	Father dies on Christmas Day.
1994	Wins third consecutive AL strikeout crown.
1995	Wins Cy Young Award, leading majors in strikeouts and ERA.
1996	Misses most of season with back injury.
1998	Traded to Houston Astros on July 31. Signs with Arizona Diamondbacks on November 30.

Statistics

Montreal Expos, Seattle Mariners, Houston Astros

Year	Team	W	L	PCT	ERA	G	GS	CG	IP	H	BB	SO	SHO
1988	Mon N	3	0	1.000	2.42	4	4	1	26	23	7	25	0
1989	Mon	0	4	.000	6.67	7	6	0	29	29	26	26	0
	Sea A	7	9	.438	4.40	22	22	2	131	118	70	104	0
	Total	7	13	.350	4.78	29	28	2	160	147	96	160	0
1990		14	11	.560	3.65	33	33	5	219	174	120	194	2
1991		13	10	.565	3.98	33	33	2	201	151	152	228	1
1992		12	14	.462	3.77	31	31	6	210	154	144	241	2
1993		19	8	.704	3.24	35	34	10	255	185	99	308	3
1994		13	6	.682	3.19	23	23	9	172	132	72	204	4
1995		18	2	.900	2.48	30	30	6	214	159	65	294	3
1996		5	0	1.000	3.67	14	8	0	61	48	25	85	0
1997		20	4	.833	2.28	30	29	5	213	147	77	291	2
1998	Sea	9	10	.474	4.33	23	23	6	160	146	60	213	2
	Hou N	10	1	.909	1.28	11	11	4	84	57	26	116	4
	Total	19	11	.633	3.30	34	34	10	244	213	86	329	6
Totals		**143**	**79**	**.644**	**3.36**	**296**	**287**	**56**	**1978**	**1533**	**943**	**2329**	**23**

Further Reading

Christopher, Matt. *On the Mound with Randy Johnson.* Boston: Little, Brown and Company, 1998.

Goodman, Michael E. *Seattle Mariners: AL West.* Mankato, MN: Creative Education, 1992.

House, Tom. *Fit to Pitch.* Champaign, IL: Human Kinetics, 1996.

Kelley, Brent P. *100 Greatest Pitchers.* New York: Crescent Books/Crown, 1988.

Stewart, Mark and Mark Friedman (ed.) *Randy Johnson: The Big Unit.* Chicago: Children's Press, 1998.

Young, Ken. *Cy Young Award Winners.* New York: Walker and Co., 1994.

Index

Armstrong, Chuck, 51
Astrodome, 53
Blowers, Mike, 41
Boggs, Wade, 30
Bosio, Chris, 41
Bradley, Scott, 31
Brown, Kevin, 55
Buford, Damon, 12
Buhner, Jay, 11, 41, 50, 53
Clemens, Roger, 13
Colangelo, Jerry, 55
Contreras, Nardi, 49
Dedeaux, Rod, 18
DeGarmo, Chris, 39
East Bay Athletic Conference, 17
Fassero, Jeff, 49, 50
Fielder, Cecil, 31
Griffey, Ken Jr., 30, 42–44, 50–53
Harris, Gene, 30
Heath, Mike, 32
Hibbard, Greg, 41
Hoff, Eric, 17, 18
Holman, Brian, 26, 30
House, Tom, 34
Hudler, Rex, 42
Jacobs Field, 52
Jamestown, New York, 21
Janus, Bud, 21
Johnson, Carol, 15, 26, 56
Johnson, Lisa, 35, 38
Johnson, Randy
  childhood, 15–19
  drafted by Montreal Expos, 19
  earns Cy Young Award, 10, 44
  picked by Atlanta Braves, 18
  signs with Arizona Diamondbacks, 55
  traded to Houston Astros, 53
  traded to Seattle Mariners, 30
Johnson, Rollen, 9, 15, 16, 34
Johnson, Samantha, 38
Johnson, Tanner Hollen, 47
Johnson, Willow, 55
Kerrigan, Joe, 23, 24, 29
Kingdome, 12, 31, 32, 39, 50
Koufax, Sandy, 23
Langston, Mark, 30, 37
Lee, Geddy, 39
Lemon, Chet, 32
Leyritz, Jim, 42
Livermore, California, 15
Martinez, Edgar, 50
Moyer, Jamie, 49
Mussina, Mike, 50
Petrocelli, Rico, 22, 23
Phillips, Tony, 32
Piniella, Lou, 11, 12, 37, 38, 42, 48
Queensryche, 39
Rodriguez, Alex, 50, 53
Royal Stadium, 9
Rush, 39
Ryan, Nolan, 34
Seattle Times, 12
Sierra, Ruben, 44
Sorrento, Paul, 11, 50
Soundgarden, 40
Southern California, University of, 18
Thayll, Kim, 40
Torre, Joe, 48
Union Gospel Mission, Seattle, 41
Walker, Larry, 25, 48, 49
Walnut Creek, California, 15
Wilson, Dan, 41
Yankee Stadium, 30

PICTURE CREDITS

AP/Wide World Photos: pp. 8, 10, 20, 26, 28, 31, 33, 36, 40, 46, 54, 56, 58; Courtesy Arizona Diamondbacks: p. 2; Courtesy of Babe Ruth Museum: p. 43; Courtesy of Eric Hoff: pp. 16, 17; Courtesy of Todd A. Peterson: p. 22; University Microfilm Inc.: p. 24; USC Athletics: pp. 14, 18

MIKE BONNER has written about sports and sports collectibles for *Sports Collectors Digest*, *Beckett Vintage Sports*, *Sports Cards Gazette*, *Oregon Sports News*, and *Sports Map* magazine. From 1992 to 1993, Mike wrote a column about the football card hobby for *Tuff Stuff* magazine. In 1993, Mike solved the mystery of the player on the fabled 1890s Mayo "Anonymous" football card, a hobby landmark.

Mike's 1995 book, *Collecting Football Cards, a Complete Guide*, is a Krause Publications title and is widely acknowledged as the best work on the subject to date. Mike has also authored two other books in the Chelsea House Sports Legends series, on NBA forward Shawn Kemp and NHL hockey star Paul Kariya.

A graduate of the University of Oregon, Mike lives in Eugene, Oregon, and is married to the former Carol Kleinheksel. Mike and Carol have one daughter, Karen.

JIM MURRAY, who passed away in 1998, was a veteran sports columnist of the *Los Angeles Times*, and one of America's most acclaimed writers. He was named "America's Best Sportswriter" by the National Association of Sportscasters and Sportswriters 14 times, was awarded the Red Smith Award, and was twice winner of the National Headliner Award. In addition, he was awarded the J. G. Taylor Spink Award in 1987 for "meritorious contributions to baseball writing." With this award came his 1988 induction into the National Baseball Hall of Fame in Cooperstown, New York. In 1990, Jim Murray was awarded the Pulitzer Prize for Commentary.

EARL WEAVER is the winningest manager in the Baltimore Orioles' history by a wide margin. He compiled 1,480 victories in his 17 years at the helm. After managing eight different minor league teams, he was given the chance to lead the Orioles in 1968. Under his leadership the Orioles finished lower than second place in the American League East only four times in 17 years. One of only 12 managers in big league history to have managed in four or more World Series, Earl was named Manager of the Year in 1979. The popular Weaver had his number, 5, retired in 1982, joining Brooks Robinson, Frank Robinson, and Jim Palmer, whose numbers were retired previously. Earl Weaver continues his association with the professional baseball scene by writing, broadcasting, and coaching.

DATE DUE			
MAR 28			
GAYLORD No. 2333			PRINTED IN U.S.A.